ERROLL

by
Hannah Shaw

ERROLL
A RED FOX BOOK 978 1 862 30447 5

First published in Great Britain by Jonathan Cape,
an imprint of Random House Children's Books
A Random House Group Company

Jonathan Cape edition published 2009
Red Fox edition published 2010

1 3 5 7 9 10 8 6 4 2

Red Fox Books are published by Random House Children's Books,
61–63 Uxbridge Road, London W5 5SA

www.kidsatrandomhouse.co.uk
www.rbooks.co.uk

Addresses for companies within The Random House Group Limited
can be found at: www.randomhouse.co.uk/offices.htm

THE RANDOM HOUSE GROUP
Limited Reg. No. 954009

A CIP catalogue record for
this book is available
from the British Library.

Printed in China

For
Ma & Pa

NEW
Nutti Nutts

NEW
Nutti Nutts

NEW
Nutti Nutts

NEW
Nutti Nutts

NEW
Nutti Nutts

NEW
Nutti Nutts

NEW
Nutti Nutts

NEW
Nutti Nutts

NEW
Nutti Nutts

NEW
Nutti Nutts

NEW
BUY ME NOW!
Nutti Nutts
Nutti Nutts
Nutti Nutts
Nutti Nutts
Nutti Nutts
Nutti Nutts
Nutti Nutts

The nicest
Nutti Nutts!

One day, Bob found a squirrel in his packet of nuts.

"**Crikes!**" yelled Bob.

"*Yikes!*" squeaked the squirrel.

Bob was sure that squirrels didn't usually talk, so this one must be rather *special.*

"I'm Bob," said Bob eagerly. **"What's your name?"**

"I'm Erroll," replied the squirrel with a t o o t h y grin.

Bob could only imagine how
Erroll had got inside
the packet of nuts in the
first place . . .

"You must be hungry after all that," said Bob.

So he made Erroll a peanut-butter sandwich.
And another . . .
and another . . .

"I like peanut butter, too," said Bob politely.

Erroll **stuffed** his face, spraying crumbs everywhere.

Soon he was covered from **head to toe** in peanut butter.

"**You need a bath!**" said Bob.
But Erroll didn't seem to like water.

"**It's got bubbles,**" said Bob.
But Erroll didn't seem
to like bubbles, either.

In the end, Bob tried cleaning Erroll
with his mum's toothbrush . . .

It took a **very** long time to catch Erroll after that . . .

Finally, Bob cornered him.

A trail of

dirty

paw

prints

led him all the way to the top
of Mum's favourite curtains,
where Erroll was swinging
dangerously.

"If you like climbing so much, there's a big tree in our garden," said Bob, hoping Erroll would make less mess outside.

Erroll scrambled up the tree as quick as a flash. He sat at the top waiting for Bob.

"It's a very long way down," said Bob, trying not to sound scared.

"Oh no, I'm stuck," he wailed a few moments later.

Luckily, Erroll was there
to help him climb down safely.

Back on the ground,
Bob could hear his mum shouting.
She sounded **very cross**.

"**Look at this mess!**
What on *earth* have you been doing?"
"**It was Erroll,**" said Bob.

"And *who* is Erroll?" asked his mum.

"**He's the talking squirrel
that I found in my packet of nuts.**"

"Don't tell fibs!"
said Bob's mum.
"There's no such thing
as a talking . . ."

"Hallo," said Erroll.

"Aggghhhhh!"
cried Bob's mum.

Bob told his mum everything.

When she had
calmed down,
she said that Erroll
would have to go
back home.

"Not back in the packet!"
said Bob in dismay.

"No, back to the woods!"
said his mum.

Bob was sad that Erroll was going home, even if he had got him into lots of trouble.

He made Erroll a **triple-mega** peanut-butter sandwich as a goodbye present.

"Goodbye, Erroll," said Bob. And when his mum wasn't looking, he whispered, "Come back and visit any time!"

"Bye-bye, Bob," said Erroll.

Erroll's friends were extremely pleased to see him again.

He told them all about his adventures with his new friend Bob.

Nut-Store

The next day, Bob had **muesli** for breakfast . . .

If you liked **Erroll**,
you'll love Evil Weasel!

Weasel is evil, measly and very rich. When he throws a big party to show off to everyone, he can't understand why none of his guests turn up...

Could it be that Weasel is bad at being a friend?

Being EVIL is easy...
But can Weasel be good?

EViL
WeaseL
Hannah Shaw

"Notable new illustrator, Hannah Shaw, fills the pages with event"
Sunday Times

"Smartly illustrated and told in a light, confident style"
Observer

Winner of the Cambridgeshire Children's Picture Book Award 2009